FIREFIGHTER'S
Night Before Christmas

FIREFIGHTER'S
Night Before Christmas

By Kimbra Cutlip
Illustrated by James Rice

PELICAN PUBLISHING COMPANY
Gretna 2002

For any firefighter and rescue worker
who has ever had to pull a holiday shift,
with special thanks to Kenny Delorenzo and
Paul Hollis

The word "Pelican" and the depiction of a pelican are trademarks
of Pelican Publishing Company, Inc., and are registered
in the U.S. Patent and Trademark Office.

Library of Congress Cataloging-in-Publication Data

Cutlip, Kimbra L.
  Firefighter's night before Christmas / by Kimbra Cutlip ; illustrated by James Rice.
    p. cm.
  Summary: In the style of Clement Moore's well-known poem, the firefighters from Firehouse One receive a visit from Ol' Sergeant Nick, who leaves them lots of surprises, including a shiny new pumper truck, while they are putting out a fire on Christmas Eve.
  ISBN 1-58980-054-0 (hardcover : alk. paper)
  1. Fire fighters—Juvenile poetry. 2. Santa Claus—Juvenile poetry. 3. Christmas—Juvenile poetry. 4. Children's poetry, American. [1. Fire fighters—Poetry. 2. Santa Claus—Poetry. 3. Christmas—Poetry. 4. American Poetry. 5. Narrative poetry.] I. Rice, James, ill. II. Title.
  PS3553.U845 F47 2002
  811'.54—dc21

                                          2002005669

Printed in Korea

Published by Pelican Publishing Company, Inc.
1000 Burmaster Street, Gretna, Louisiana 70053

FIREFIGHTER'S NIGHT BEFORE CHRISTMAS

'Twas the Christmas Eve shift at Firehouse One,
And the day had been quiet, not one single run.

Paul had played Santa for kids in the town,
Who had snapped his suspenders and pulled his beard down.
While Marguerite dressed as an elf and gave toys,
Rosie the medic tried to herd little boys.

Big Bob had cooked up some chili real hot,
For a three-alarm supper in a five-gallon pot.
We were dishing out seconds for a late-night round two
With some cops on the beat who had nothing to do.

They checked in to see all the unlucky stiffs,
Who, like them, were pulling the Christmas Eve shift.
They were making to leave and get back to their route,
When Kenny yelled over, "Hey, come check this out!"

"There's a truck with its Mars light gyrating away
And a Christmas tune playing on the siren's PA.
Strobe lights are flashing and everything's going,
And I know it sounds crazy, but the ladder pipe's
  snowing."

Sure enough at the door to the ladder-truck bay
Was an aerial rig with lights on display.
The tower was covered with red and green light,
And a tree at the top glittered into the night.

"Jingle Bells" blared from the siren real loud,
And the nozzle sprayed snow in the air like a cloud.
"Well, here's our white Christmas," I said through the clatter.
Then a frosty old firefighter dashed up the ladder.

He jumped to the roof like a smoke-eating pro,
And into the stove vent he squeezed one big toe.
Then he stuffed all the rest of himself down there too,
And we ran to the kitchen to see what he'd do.

When he fell on the stove in his red turnout gear,
The grin on his face nearly stretched ear to ear.
There was soot in the wrinkles that framed his blue eyes,
And his ash-colored beard made him look old and wise.

A pipe in his pocket stuck out just a bit,
And he looked at it fondly—"Been trying to quit."
On his helmet the badge number read "Zero North,"
And he winked a sly wink as we stared back and forth.

"That smells like fine chili—could I have a taste?
Dispatch has been running me—no time to waste."
Before we could answer, he finished it all.
Then the alarm went off—it was time for a call.

We jumped in our boots as we'd all done before,
But a Christmas Eve call was different for sure.
Visions of families flashed in our heads,
While all of us hoped ours were safe in their beds.

Dispatch told us as we rolled out the door
Some tree lights caught fire at a furniture store.
When we got there the flames had spread through the place,
So the captain radioed for help with the blaze.

"Engine One on the scene," he reported, "side one.
Smoke and fire showing"—this was no easy run.
He said, "Fill the box—we'll need help here fast,"
As we laid an attack line and started to blast.

The battalion chief called for two alarms more!
And we knew if we hustled we might save the store.
From the deck guns and pipes we had water flowing,
And soon, through the smoke, white steam started showing.

We worked through the night to save what we could,
And when it was done, we all felt pretty good.
The storefront was gone but we saved the warehouse,
And no one was injured, not even a mouse.

We wearily loaded our hose in the bed,
But we knew there was plenty of work left ahead.
To get back in service we'd tend to it all.
We had to be ready when we got the next call.

We rolled into the station with dawn on the rise
And couldn't believe what greeted our eyes.
Ours was the only yard that had snow,
And a shiny new pumper sat ready to go.

The red firefighter must have been mighty swift.
I suspect that his truck had been loaded with gifts.
While we were gone he had laid out surprises
And filled up the station with gifts of all sizes.

There were new socks for Louie, whose feet always stunk.
For all of her books, Rosie got a new trunk.
Eddie and Paul got laptops and games,
And a case of car wax was a big thrill for James.

There was a fancy new grill for our cook, big Bob,
And steaks in the freezer to help with the job.
Spot, the house dog, got a collar in red,
And Stretch got a specially extralong bed.

And there in the rec room, the whole company
Found new lounging chairs and a flat-screen TV.
The bill for the cable was paid for the year.
With 200 channels—what fights we will hear!

Dog tired and dirty, we couldn't turn in.
There was too much to look at, too much to take in.
So we broke out the grill and cooked up some steak.
We had pulled Christmas shift—it was our lucky break.

Of course, the lieutenant had work left to do.
On his desk was the log book and paperwork too.
The night wasn't over until it was done.
But it seems the old man had logged in our run.

He'd listed our names and checked them off twice,
And next to each one he wrote "naughty" or "nice."
Headquarters will say we were playing a trick,
But he signed, "Merry Christmas, from Ol' Sergeant Nick."